I0749405

HIDDEN REALMS

Three short stories of the paranormal and the unknown, to delight, chill, and make you wonder.

By

Marta Moran Bishop

&

Patricia Moran

Crowe Press

Cover Art R. Jade Lazlow

This collection of short stories is dedicated to my mother, Patricia Moran, who wrote the beginnings of two of the three stories and gave me my love of reading and writing.

THE OTHER SIDE

Patricia Moran

&

Marta Moran Bishop

Crowe Press

CHAPTER ONE

Isle's long silver hair flowed around her with a life of its own. It danced with each graceful step she took. Sometimes it appeared as a hooded cape as it sat in waves across her shoulders and down her back. At other times, it was a veil hiding her face making her disappear in the leaves of a tree or, like wings, it fanned out riding the breeze. Edward delighted in its beauty. His hands ached to touch the silky, brilliant locks—especially when it cocooned her oval face. For when it did, her startling silver-blue eyes seared into the depths of his soul. Her rosy cheeks and ruby lips nearly begged to be kissed, yet he paused.

"Edward," she said as she took his rough, weather-beaten hand into hers. "Life is different here than in your world. We have had a few others cross over and tell us stories of your world, though it has been many years since anyone came. The last one passed over the rainbow bridge when I was just a child."

Interrupting, he said, "Isle it is unseemly for me to hold hands with you and feel as I do about you, for I am growing old and you are barely into your womanhood. You're still almost a child." He blushed and began to pull his hand from hers. He ached to leave it there, yet felt it an unholy thing, for he believed her to be very young. "I never felt an attraction for young girls, and I'm finding it very embarrassing. It feels an evil thing the way I feel about you, yet my heart sings when you're near."

He looked confused. Maybe this world was like many of the countries in his world where girls were considered adults when they were still children.

"I am older than you think, Edward. We are a long-lived race, dearest. Dearest, for that is what you are to me, and so that is what I will call you. Our people don't begin to appear old until we are at the end and the time of our leaving this world has grown close. If the truth be told, I'm a bit older than you are regardless of my youthful appearance."

"Isle, how can that be so? I know this world is different, if in fact it isn't a dream. But for you to say you're older is difficult for me to believe, though I know you wouldn't lie. If I'm not dreaming, perhaps I'm delusional?"

"You aren't dreaming, nor are you delusional. I can promise you that. Our souls have been entwined since the dawn of time, and at my birth it was spoken that we would meet."

"This isn't my world, Isle, even if I feel as if it's my home."

"It is your home, Edward. It always has been. You only had to allow yourself to find it. If you don't believe me, we could walk down to the river, and you can see the changes that have already begun in you."

"What do you mean?" he asked sharply, maybe a bit too sharply if truth were told, but he'd been startled.

"When did your hair turn silver?" she asked.

That's an odd question, but I'll answer anyway, he thought. "I think I was about five or six if I remember correctly. The doctors thought losing my parents must have brought it on. They called it premature graying, looked at me oddly, and did many tests. I can't tell you the results. All I know is I went back to the orphanage soon after, and that was the end of it, except for the names the other children called me."

"Have you noticed you have more of a spring in your step and feel lighter of foot since you got here? Edward, you are one of us whether you believe it or not. I don't know how you ended up in the other world. Maybe the elders do."

The air smelled of lavender, roses, and lilacs. They listened to the music of the brook as it rippled and jumped over the rocks on its way downstream as they walked quietly hand in hand to the village. Just over the hill, Edward gasped with the beauty of the city before him. Isle had called it her village, but the jewel colored buildings lit the sky, making their own rainbow against the shimmering lake in front of them.

Their feet were nearly silent on the quaint wooden bridge as they crossed from the path to the city. Flutes, harps, violins, and pianos could be heard the closer they came to the gates. Even the occasional guitar, horn, and drum could be heard. Unlike many cities of earth, all its streets were lined with trees and flowers. He didn't see any sign of man's desecration of property. No soiled food wrappers, empty soda cans, or dog droppings. Here and there in small courtyards stood a table or two, a coffee urn, a decanter of tea, and sometimes he saw a keg of beer spouted and ready to pour.

CHAPTER TWO

"Are you thirsty, Edward?" Isle asked as she led him into one of the courtyards. "It has been a long walk."

"Yes, I guess I am, Isle. I didn't even realize I was until you mentioned it."

"Would you like something cold or hot?"

"Oh, cold, please."

"Beer, or lemonade?" She asked him, leading him to a small credenza under the trees. "I'm going to have a lemonade, but they have incredible beer here." A small smile lit her face as she poured herself a lemonade and waited for his answer.

"I think lemonade. It seems a bit early in the day for beer. Yes, lemonade." He held a glass out for her to pour the fresh lemonade into it.

The lemonade shimmered in the crystal glasses as they carried it to a table buried under a canopy of ivy. As he pulled out her chair, he once again yearned to touch the shimmering silver of her cascading hair. Instead, he took the seat across from her, gazed into her eyes, and asked, "Isle, who do we pay?"

She looked back at him quizzically. "What do you mean when you say 'pay,' Edward?"

"For our lemonade, of course, shouldn't we exchange money with whoever owns this place?

"Pay!" she said, her lovely face a mask of confusion. "I don't understand that word, dearest."

Out of his pocket, Edward pulled his wallet. He took out a dollar bill and handed it to her.

She stared at it, turning it over, touching and tracing the artwork. Suddenly she looked up with a wide look of understanding on her face. "Oh Edward, I remember now. It has been so long since we talked of money here. I was a little girl the last time it was discussed. We don't use money, dearest. We have no need of it."

His face darkened a bit. Now he was unable to understand her. "How do you compensate people without money? Do you use gold or silver?"

"No, it isn't about money here. We have no need of it."

"Then how do the people who own this café pay for the things they offer here? Who pays for the lemons? How do they get them?"

Now she was confused again. "What's a café?"

He sat quietly, finally realizing she wasn't teasing him but fearfully honest. He recognized just how alien this world was from all he knew.

"Is this someone's home, Isle?" he asked quietly.

"Of course it is, Edward. We all have something we share with each other. Some have places for someone to eat, others are like this. Some people make quilts, curtains, or buggies. Each person offers what they do best, and an honest exchange is made."

"What will we exchange here, Isle?"

"Oh silly, it wouldn't be here necessarily. It isn't a flat out barter system. Yes, I read those histories. It has just been such an exceedingly long time. When our friends can use something of equal value, it will be theirs. We don't cheat each other or shirk our duties. Each of us gives the best we have in us. It works out. You'll see."

He sat there looking at her, and then down at the dollar bill lying on the table. His glance moved around the flower lined courtyard to the street, where the music was playing, and finally back to her face. He searched it for a long time, maybe too long, for he felt the presence of a way of life he didn't feel he could ever understand. Finally, he said to her softly, "Isle, I must leave them something. I don't know how to live this way. You say I'll learn, but I feel like a thief or a communist here. What can I leave?"

Her expression filled with puzzlement. She studied him. "Dearest, what's a thief? What's a communist? I read your face, your heart, and I know these are not good things."

"A thief takes something and leaves nothing, Isle. Please, what can I leave?"

CHAPTER THREE

Her expression grew solemn as she studied his grim face. Then she jumped up. "Wait here. I'll be right back." She hurried to the door of the home.

Edward sat still and stared at the glass in his hand, his dollar bill lying on the polished maple table, the laurel and ivy leaves surrounding them, and waited. His thoughts were grim and he felt unhappy, even when he saw the loveliness of Isle walk back toward him with an older gentleman. He stood, but he felt lost.

"This is Mr. Mattahal, Edward. He lives here," her lovely voice barely whispered.

The older gentleman held out his hand. Edward took it, and solemnly the two men shook hands.

"Isle tells me that you feel the need to offer something to me now." Mr. Mattahal said, his voice full of a kind wariness. "It's not the normal way of things, sir, but if you must do this, I will try to accommodate you," he said with a smile.

"Yes, sir, I will value it enormously if you'd allow me to offer you something now. What can I do or give you?"

Mr. Mattahal stood there for a moment, completely dumbfounded. He'd understood what Isle told him but was uncomfortable with the entire idea. He felt as much a fish out of water as Edward did at the moment, so he stood gazing at the younger man. At last, he glanced down at the table and saw the leather wallet open and the new bill lying out face up, just as Isle had left it after inspecting it. "I like this. It would look splendid in the frame I received the other day. My wife would like it too. Would you feel comfortable giving it to me?" he asked, holding the one-dollar bill in his hand.

"Are you sure?" Edward said, for, in his world, one dollar bought much more than two glasses of lemonade, no matter how fine it was.

"Young man, I have never seen anything like this, so to me it would be a treasure indeed," replied

Mr. Mattahal coolly, feeling a tiny bit insulted by this odd man in front of him. Then with a sigh, his kind heart felt pity instead for the depth of hurt and heartache that must exist in the world Edward came from.

The bargain struck and each man felt a bit more content, if only because the issue had been resolved. Neither truly comfortable with the ending though. The older man turned and went back into his home and Edward sat staring, with a strange look on his face. While the two men had been talking, Isle cleaned the glasses and wiped down the table for the next person who might stop here. She looked up at Edward plaintively, for she now feared losing him. His face was a mask of grief and lack of understanding of their way of life.

"Isle, I need to go back. I can't stay here. I wish I could, but I just can't," he said.

"Edward, darling man, can you not give it more time?"

CHAPTER FOUR

"No, I don't think so. Not yet. I need to go back and think. Maybe I'll be able to figure it out and come back. Right now, I don't know. I do know I love you, and I always will, but I just can't stay," he said as they walked out of the courtyard and down the street to the bridge.

No matter how many times she took his hand, he released it and walked on a little faster through the fields of flowers and past the singing brook. Soon he was nearly running. He felt terrible. His world had been turned upside down, and he was more afraid than he'd ever been. He felt like he'd lose himself if he stayed.

When they reached the cliff, he stopped and turned to her. Her silver hair tangled from the run, her breath short, and her face dark and frightened. She too felt the loss. Though her loss was different, it was the loss of the only love she had ever known or wanted. It was the loss of all that had been promised her from birth. His hand raised to her cheek and touched it softly, gently caressing the length of her jaw, running his finger across her lips and his eyes memorizing every line of her.

She took his hand, kissed his rough fingers, and let her mouth rest on his palm. She put her hands on each side of his face and pulled his head to her. Lips meeting, she kissed him. "Please, Edward, must you go? Can't you stay just a little longer?"

With a last look at her, he picked up his hat from the ground where it had fallen when he arrived before he met Isle and turned toward the cliff. Tears slide down both of their cheeks and welled in their eyes, each of them already ached from loss.

"Edward, it might not be possible to come back. No one has ever been able to before. Are you sure?"

He kept his back to her, for he couldn't bear to see her face. His longing already deep, he answered, "I don't know if I could come back anyway, no matter how much I long to, no matter how much our souls are tied. I don't know if I can live here."

With a sigh, he began walking toward the cliff and disappeared.

CHAPTER FIVE

I honestly don't know what made me think of him tonight. After all, he's been dead and gone for almost two years now. Well, at least he's been gone. Nobody knows for sure if he's dead or not. I mean, they never found his body or anything, but then, nobody ever actually looked particularly hard either.

He was just a kind of goofy old guy who used to live in this neighborhood. Crazy Ed, they called him. The whole gang of us used to make fun of him when we had nothing else to do. It never actually got us anywhere. You see, Ed didn't pay us no never mind. He never got mad or nothing. He just looked sort of sad and hurt and went on humming his funny little song. He would sit, staring at the wall at the end of the alley. My folks told me that long ago he used to have a terrific job downtown until he disappeared for a couple of days. When he got back, all he did was sit on this ashcan, and stare at the wall. He never hurt nobody and no one cared much about him. It seemed he spent all his time in this alley. At least I never saw him anywhere else.

The funny thing about old Ed was that he seemed real intelligent, and he talked to us about the war, the neighborhood, and all kinds of things. I mean he was really educated. He wasn't the same as most people in the neighborhood. Most folks here work hard at the local factory six days a week, as their fathers did before them, and most had never gotten past the eighth grade either.

The thing about Ed was he had that kick about sitting in this alley. Funny, I feel quite close to him tonight sitting here on Ed's ashcan looking down at the dirty old wall, just like Ed did.

Seeing as he's been gone quite a long time now, I expect he wouldn't mind me telling you a story he told me one day.

CHAPTER SIX

Do you remember the summer of nineteen hundred and sixty-five, when I broke my leg, and how after that I'd never join in when the other kids were making fun of old Ed? Well, while I was laid up with my leg in a cast. I spent a bit of time down here with old Ed. It was during that time he told me the story of this here alley and that dirty old wall.

It was a night a lot like tonight is, kind of warm, with a little moonlight around, and the air sort of soft. It seemed quiet, just like it does now. I'd been sitting here with Ed for a while talking about things in general and griping about missing out on all the fun because of my bum leg, when he looked at me real steady for a few minutes. Then he started to talk. I swear the story he told me was so crazy, you couldn't believe it, but it was obvious that Ed believed it.

He told me how he used to be a big, hot shot lawyer down in the loop, and he had a client who lived up the hill from here. One morning the weather was so fine, he parked a block down from here, got himself a coffee and decided to walk the rest of the way up to his client's house.

"Johnny, the sky was so blue that day. Only a few picturesque clouds drifted across the sky. There was just enough of a breeze that day to grab my hat right off my head and cause it to bounce a little down the street and finally sail into this alley," Ed said to me. "I'd been chasing that dang hat for a few minutes, nearly catching it several times only to have it bounce again and sail on, until it finally came to a stop right here in front of this wall. I bent down to pick it up, and the wall opened up."

No, I swear that's what he said. The wall opened just like a gate and beyond it were green grass, trees, and flowers everywhere. Naturally he was surprised. I mean, here in this neighborhood anybody would be surprised to see grass, trees, and flowers. It isn't as if this in one of the swank neighborhoods, just a regular factory neighborhood. A bit rough some days, but not like Humboldt Park or Wicker Park either.

Anyway, Ed told me he just up and walked through the opening in the wall and found himself in another world. Now mind you, he said he didn't know it was another world at first. He thought it was a park he hadn't known was there.

Anyway, he told me it was warm there, not hot, and as he walked he stopped feeling tired, just a little sleepy. He had long since forgotten his meeting with the client, sat down on the grass under a tree, and just enjoyed the day. He sat there and listened to the birds singing to each other, the coo of the mourning dove, and the chirp of the crickets. The air was soft, warm, and somewhere off in the distance he heard the sound of water running.

"I expect I dozed a bit then, Johnny, for I woke to the sound of a red cardinal sitting on my chest singing its heart out," he said. "I noticed that the sun was high in the sky, and I was hungry. I sat up and looked at my watch, but it had stopped, and somehow I had lost all track of which way I had come into the park. I was in a real pickle," he said with a chuckle.

Ed went on with his story, and I just sat there both fascinated and thinking it was the craziest story I had ever heard. Anyway, Ed went on with his story, and he didn't seem to notice the odd look I'm sure I had on my face. He just continued talking in that quiet voice of his.

"There I was in some strange park, with no idea how to get out or where I could find something to eat. I looked around. To the right of me was a forest of trees and to the left a hill. I could hear the sound of water coming from the other side of the hill. I began to get a bit worried, but before I could become truly scared, something happened which changed my whole life. A young girl came walking through the trees carrying a small wicker basket.

"She wasn't young like you are, Johnny, nor what many would call stunning, but to me she was the most beautiful girl I had ever seen. She walked right up to me with no fear in her bearing and acted as if she had been expecting me for a long time. After placing the basket on the ground, she sat next to me and took my hand.

"'Edward,' she said simply, as if we had always known each other.

"Now, the next part," he said, "was like a dream, or the remembering of it was the dream. I couldn't really say. She was dressed in some kind of shimmering, glistening, chiffony thing. Now, Johnny, I don't know women's clothing, but it looked to me as if she were a Greek goddess. Her clothes reminded me of those that are sculpted on the statues in the museum.

"Her eyes were a light silver and her hair long, thick, and a shining pewter color. Her voice tinkled when she spoke, and there was a hint of laughter in her words—not the kind of jeering laughter, more of a happiness that brimmed over into life itself. Her name was Isle.

"As she talked, she opened the basket and pulled out a plate of grapes the size of plums and handed them to me. When I remarked about their size, Isle told me they grew on the bushes near her hamlet. Now, Johnny," Ed said, "I don't know how long Isle and I sat there and talked, because it was the sweetest moment of my entire life. Soon the sun moved a little closer to the horizon, and Isle placed the plates and glasses back into her basket and stood. She took my hand and asked me if I wanted to visit her village and meet her people.

"The closer we came to the village, the louder the sound of pure, sweet, voices filled the air. Laughter from children filled the grassy path. All the people I saw as we walked along appeared to be industrious, yet none seemed to be in a hurry, nor did anyone act as if they were in charge of the rest. Instead, they worked together, each of them doing the thing that made them happy and fulfilled a needed task in the village.

CHAPTER SEVEN

"It was the most beautiful place I had ever seen, Johnny. Ed said with a hint of sorrow in his voice. Everyone dressed much like Isle did, though the men's tunics were shorter than the women's. The air held the scent of nectar, pine, and the sea. It was so fresh and pure as if mankind had never stepped into this place to ruin it with their cars, factories, coal, soot, and garbage. I saw no police stations, hospitals, court houses, or policemen, and I asked Isle about this as we walked through the village hand in hand.

It was odd, Johnny. She didn't understand war, hate, crime, death, or sickness and seemed genuinely perplexed at the thought of all these things. I could tell that the entire concept was something entirely beyond her ability to comprehend.

That evening she took me to a performance at an enormous open-air theatre. Many people took turns playing music or acting out a part in small theatre productions, and we sat under the stars and watched. It was the most magical show of my life. It didn't contain heartache, only the joy of life.

After the show, everyone sang and danced. The stars hung low, and moonlight lit the sky. Fireflies soared in and out of the dancers, sometimes landing on an arm or the pewter hair of one of the villagers. It was exceedingly strange, Johnny, that no one asked me my name or treated me as if I was different from them. It was as if they had always known me. They all acted like I'd always lived in the village. I've never felt so welcome, not even when I was a young boy, before the war.

The next day we walked through the village. I began to look for places of business. There appeared to be many outdoor cafés, and she asked if I was thirsty, so we stopped at one. Isle went to a side board near an outdoor pump and poured us a glass of lemonade. As we sat at the table and drank, I realized it was the most refreshing lemonade I'd ever tasted. There was a tartness to it that quenched one's thirst like nothing I'd ever had before. When we were finished, I pulled my wallet and some coins from my pocket to pay. Johnny, Isle looked at it as if it was some strange type of art. She turned it over in her hand and examined the pyramid and eye on the back of the bill before she carefully handed it back to me.

She tried to explain their culture to me, Johnny, and I didn't understand it. I was so uncomfortable I felt like a thief or a communist. I finally convinced her that I needed to reciprocate, and she got the owner of the house to come out. He didn't understand what I wanted and seemed as uncomfortable with it as Isle was, but he was a kind gentleman and agreed to trade with me. He took a one dollar bill, which he told me he would frame. I tell you, boy, I was in extreme distress. I practically ran out of there, and as I ran, I noticed that in front of each house stood a few tables. I finally understood the place we stopped at wasn't a café at all. It was someone's home. I tried to explain money and commerce to Isle, but she found the notion funny. She asked me why there was a need to buy things when the earth held such bounty.

I'm telling you, Johnny, no one went hungry, each person worked at the things they were best at and loved to do. Every man, woman, and child helped each other with those tasks that needed more than one or two people. Greed just wasn't in their nature.

I felt as if somehow, I had passed straight through to heaven. In some strange way, I knew Isle and I had always been together. That's when I blew it, Johnny. She asked me to stay with her. Her silver eyes stared straight into my heart as she told me she had always loved me.

I was confused. It felt like some sort of communist trap, even though I knew it wasn't. I felt I wasn't good enough for her world or for her love, and I said I wanted to go back."

Then Ed began crying. I don't mean a bit of moisture in his eyes, but out and out sobbing as if his heart had broken. I swear I just sat there dumbfounded wanting to help him, but I didn't believe his story. Nor did I know what to do for him.

"Ed, why did you come back?" I asked

CHAPTER EIGHT

At first, he didn't answer. He only sobbed and then said, "I couldn't even say goodbye as I took my last look at her, walked through the wall, and back into this world. It was the hardest thing I ever did. The moment the wall closed, and I could no longer see Isle, I knew I'd made a mistake. I banged on the wall screaming for it to open until a police officer heard me. I fought him hard, and then I broke. When his back-up came, they forced me into the wagon and took me to the hospital.

I spent weeks in that hospital, doped up on some mighty strange drugs. No one believed me, and I spent day after day in talk therapy.

At long last, I figured that my only way out of the hospital was to let them think I was 'better.'

So I pretended it was all because I'd been working too hard. Finally, one day they let me out of the hospital.

I went back to my law business, but it all seemed wrong—the dirt and the noise of the city, the murky deals, and greedy people. Bankers, thieves, everyone wanting to 'get their hands in the pie.' I couldn't do it anymore."

I'm telling you he sat there on this old ashcan and cried like a baby. It seems the last blow to him and his old life came when the war in Vietnam broke out and the young men began dying on the battlefield all to fight communism, the idea of communism being one of the reasons he felt he had run away from Isle's world. There was so much sickness of both body and spirit, and it began to seep into his bones. After he finished talking about the current war, he told me he walked out of his life and never looked back. He just came back to this alley, not knowing what happened to his house, his business, or anything. He just sat here in this dirty alley waiting.

"What do you do here Ed? I asked.

"I stand for a while, then sit on this old ash can and watch that dirty brick wall, and I wait for it to open up again."

"Where do you sleep, Ed?" I asked. "Where do you get your food?"

"I sleep rolled up right against the wall behind the ash can, and people throw their leftovers into that dumpster over there."

"You eat garbage?"

"Some would call it that, and some would consider it a meal fit for a king," he said plainly. "I don't leave this alley, not ever, and I am real quiet now. I won't go back to that hospital. Someday the wall will open again. It just has too. My heart is on the other side, and people can't live without their hearts."

At that point, he turned back to the wall, and I knew there wasn't anything more I would get Ed to talk about that day.

When I went back a few days later, Ed wasn't there. I thought maybe the police had taken him back to the hospital, but I called them all and no one knew what happened to old Ed.

I don't know if his story was true. I don't even know if he was once a successful lawyer downtown. All I know is that for over five years Ed was in this alley. Winter, summer, spring, and fall. It didn't matter how hot or cold it was or if it was night or day. He was here, until one day he wasn't.

The cops said he probably moved on or died someplace and no one had claimed his body. All I know is one day he was sitting here as usual, and then he was gone.

That was two years ago in nineteen hundred and sixty-seven. Maybe it's as everyone claims, and he just went away. I don't know, but I wonder.

I know it sounds crazy, but he was so sure. Maybe that wall did open again. I mean, how do we know for sure?"

THE NIGHT OF THE FAIRIES

Marta Moran Bishop

CHAPTER ONE

Astarte, leaned back against the rocks and watched the moonlight's silver glitter fill the field with a glow. She pulled her cloak up over her head to cover her red hair. That stopped the cold breeze from blowing down her neck. It had been a long day, but she could not give up the beauty of the stars, and the magic of the glow in the field beyond the cave.

The tribe didn't understand her fascination with the moon's glow. They couldn't see the fairies dance in the field after midnight. They didn't see them because they were fast asleep, dreaming of the last hunt. They woke with the dawn, broke bread, and began their day.

The women went to the fields to harvest the wild herbs and grain. Sometimes they roamed for miles before they found what they were seeking. The men of the clan spent most days hunting when the meat supply was low. At times the men were gone for days before they returned with a deer, elk, or even a sack of rabbits if they could not find anything else that day.

When the hunt was excellent, they sang songs of victory and repaired their weapons, readying them for the next hunt. It was then that the mead flowed heavily, and the air filled with male laughter as they worked. At nightfall, before they slept, they danced. Half naked, their arms heavily adorned with bands of bright feathers, and the teeth of their prey, tusks of wild boar swung from their necks, and the hollowed heads of their kill sat upon their heads, the blood dripping onto their painted faces. The sound of their chants and songs of praise to the gods filled the air.

If the hunt had been long, or the meat scarce, the men would sit together and plan the next move. The clan followed the herds, though usually they only moved twice. Once to their summer home and the second to the sea, where the warmth of the water kept the weather more temperate.

Before the cold of the winter months, the journey that would take them across the plains, over the mountains, and to the seas to trade their furs and their women with the other clans began.

Astarte knew she was coming of age, and on the next trip she would be traded.

If they moved, she would lose the beauty of the fairies dancing in the moonlight as they spread the seeds across the field. She would be traded to another tribe. She would become the property of a man from another tribe, her days filled with cooking, cleaning, sewing, mending, and taking care of one baby after another.

I don't want to marry one of the men from the tribes, she thought. I don't want to leave the fairies or this place again. Already, the clan is planning their next move. There must be a way. Why do I see the fairies and they can't? What's different in me, and why do I wish for a life beyond what I have known? If I marry, I don't want it to be a man of the clans, who cannot see the fairies, and his only thought is of the hunt, a full belly, mead to cloud his brain, and tales of adventure. The world must be more than that, or there would be no fairies.

CHAPTER TWO

Very early in life, she had learned that talking about the fairies brought about disdain from the clan.

Astarte remembered when she was little and talked about the fairies for the first time. The women had called the old mother, and for days, Astarte was given beaker after beaker of a tincture to drink. It smelled of dirt, garlic, and mule dung, and it had tasted even worse. Now she doubted if in fact there was mule dung or muck in it. Yet she remembered the odor well, a dark, musty, and vile smell. That mixture made her drowsy, her mind cloudy, and her tongue unable to form words for a days. She never talked of the things she saw in the moonlight again.

Even later, when she'd talked one of the other children into staying out to watch the moon, telling her a tale about the unique herbs that could be seen in the moonlight, she hadn't mentioned the fairies, but she waited to see if her friend saw them too.

Doeina chattered away as the two of them stood against the rocks. Eventually Doeina's babble stopped, and she became quiet. But it wasn't the night or the beauty that made Doeina silent. She had fallen asleep, wrapped in her child's cloak. Astarte never brought anyone back, but that night she watched the fairies dance until just before dawn. Then she woke Doeina. The two of them carefully snuck back into the village, and into the orphan's tent. Astarte knew then that no one except her would ever see the fairies, at least not anyone from this village.

As she watched the fairies dance in the field below, she knew they couldn't be as small as they appeared from her vantage point. I'm small for my age, she thought, and in this clan, my head barely reaches the waist of the adults. The children I grew up with now tower over me. Who am I? I don't look like anyone here, and the tribe won't talk about my mother or who she was. Did she die or just leave me here? Astarte wondered again as she had over the years since her brain had developed past childhood.

I'm afraid, she silently admitted to herself. Someone might notice the large growths on my back. I know if they marry me off at the gathering, my future mate will notice. How could he not? Will the growths become even bigger? What are they? As it is, they itch all the time now.

CHAPTER THREE

"Who am I? What am I?" Astarte whispered as she stood there in the cold night air, waiting for the fairies to come. She needed the magic badly tonight. Her mind had been terrified for weeks as her body began its changes. These weren't the normal changes of the other girls, and she dreaded what it might mean for her.

As was normal for the nights the fairies came to the meadow, she first heard the music of their flutes on the wind, and then the field below became an enchanted place of beauty. Bright colors lit the sky, and the dance began again—only tonight it called her more than it ever had before. Several times she caught herself moving toward the field, only to move back to the rocks, afraid. Yet Astarte was mesmerized, the pull too strong to overcome. Slowly, she moved out of the rocks, and as she walked closer to the field, she felt as if she glided on air. Her dark cloak fell off her shoulders. Then the back of her leather tunic felt as if it were going to explode. The pain between her shoulders grew as her body drew closer to the meadow below. A warm, sticky fluid flowed down her back, drenching her clothes.

The sweet, warm, tropical breezes of the field filled her nostrils, and her heart lifted as she drew close. She was so near now that she could see the faces of each fairy, their graceful colored wings gliding and glittering in the breezes as they halted, staring at her. Astarte stopped, the pull toward them nearly as great as the fear that froze her into place, as they looked at each other. Her heart filled with the need to join them, yet she stood and waited. The leather tunic dripped and pulled tighter across her back. The stain spread further, leaving trails of a sticky, milky substance on her tunic.

As suddenly as the flutes stopped, they began again and filled her soul with their music. The lilting melody made her ache with the need to pull off the trappings of the clan and dress in the flowing, gauzy, bright, garments of the fairies. Gone was her past and her memories of the clan. The fairy world filled her as she moved into the circle.

The fairy women gathered around her, cloaked her from the sight of the others, from the breeze, and from the world. "You are Astarte. Your mother is waiting. Her heart may now recover from her loss of you. My name is Schauna. I'm her sister," the red haired fairy said to her as she took a silver blade and cut the deerskin tunic from Astarte's body. "Your wings came late, we have been waiting for you to mature, for many a moon now." Schauna's voice was melodic as she used a soft, warm, soothing cloth, and wiped the gooey mess from Astarte's back. Soon, Astarte's wings were free of the last of the leather that clung to them. The damp cloth smelled like early morning dew, drenched in wild lavender, and relaxed her back. The agony was now gone.

Astarte stood quietly, her mind too full of questions for her to speak; instead, she let them free her long red hair, clean her soiled back, and dress her in a long, golden dress, which flowed to her small bare feet. Her new wings opened, drying in the scented breeze. Her heart full of joy, she wanted to fly and join the dance, yet knew that she would need to build up the strength of her wings. She basked in the bliss of belonging.

THE HOLLOWERS

Patricia Moran

CHAPTER ONE

That fateful day began the same as almost every other day for Jerry. "At least the rain has stopped so my bus won't be held up in traffic. So, I have one decent thing to be thankful for today," Jerry thought as he grimaced at himself in the mirror. The slight bend in his nose from the blow his father had given him as a child went unnoticed by him. "Shaving is such a chore. I remember the old days." His mind wandered back to his youth. Damn! This wasn't the way it was supposed to be as his mind drifted back to the year he dropped out of college. "What an exciting year that was," he thought.

Protests, marches, sit-ins, riots, anti-war parades, and slogans. Wow! Not that he had ever participated in any of them—it was not his style—not his thing as they said in those days, but these things were exciting to read and talk about. Anybody could get a job then, and many of his friends dropped out of school and went to work, so he followed along. It seemed the right thing to do; after all, school was a bore. There was one thing Jerry was exceptionally adept at, and that was following others. Unfortunately, he was only good at following if it was the easiest thing for him to do.

He was long on talk and short on action, so when his friends went off to form a commune, he thought about it for quite some time before taking a job as a salesman for a shoe store. "Now, that job was fun!" he said to himself. "At least until they fired me for sneaking a quick look up the women's skirts. How unfair that was," he thought for the hundredth time. "If a woman wears a short skirt, why would it be my fault for looking at what she was offering?" Even now, years later, he still didn't understand the management's problem. "If the stupid bitch hadn't complained, I would still have that job," he thought again.

From then on in it was one sales job after another, and at night on his way home, he stopped at the local pub and even joined a pool league. Day followed day, becoming years and one by one his friends married or moved away. The new crowd didn't seem his type; they were younger, and he just didn't seem to fit in. He remembered the day the bar was sold to make room for a drugstore. It was then that he lost his home away from home, and it was a blow he never quite recovered from.

CHAPTER TWO

After floating from one meaningless sales job to another, he landed his current post in "the boiler room." He hated the job but had gotten fired from so many sales jobs over the years, he felt stuck. "I hate it even if it is less of an effort than finding a new job, or heaven forbid, going back to school, and at my age too. Besides, the paycheck is steady," he told himself as he took a comb to his hair and tried combing the strands of his hair over his receding hairline, but decided the women in the secretarial pool were right—it looked stupid. "I've heard them all joke about men trying to hide their balding heads by combing their hair over them," he muttered out of the corner of his mouth, smoothing a bit of gel into the gray at his temples and pulling the back of his now graying hair into a ponytail.

Jerry didn't seem to notice what a weird combination a ponytail, graying hair, and a balding head actually were.

"I really should put a stronger bulb in here," he said to himself, knowing full well he would never get around to it. Jerry was always planning things to do on his day off, but somehow, they never got done. "What the hell—life's too short! Why spend all of it worrying about things?" he mumbled as he buttoned his rumpled white shirt as he walked out of the bathroom, to get his coat and the tie he had left on the chair in front of the TV last night. The old wide floral tie covered the small mustard stain on the front of his white shirt.

On his way out the door, he picked up his new gray suede overcoat lying on the brown and yellow checked sofa bed. With a glance, he thought as he did every day, "I should have made it this morning."

The apartment looked pretty much as it did the day he moved in fifteen years ago. He had rented it furnished and so it remained. A few cheaply framed landscapes and a floral print hung on the walls. The wallpaper with its small roses was yellowed with age. All the pictures hung just a bit too high for Jerry. He had meant to rehang them, but those plans to never amounted to much. The efficiency apartment, like many things in Jerry's life seemed a waste of time. He spent his time watching television from the faux leather recliner that sat in the corner of the room, a TV tray beside it, covered now in the remnants of last night's supper. A few beer bottles littered the floor beside it, along with an ashtray filled with the remains of a joint. The recliner was the only purchase he had made over the years. It had lost its shine, but who cared? It was still comfortable. "After all, who sees it but me?" he thought as he tossed his coat over his shoulder in what he felt gave him a James Bond look.

Before closing the door, Jerry stooped and picked up his morning newspaper, turned, closed, and locked the door. "Well, another, day another dollar," he said as he walked out the door.

Climbing down the rickety stairs of the old apartment building, overcoat slung over his shoulder, he felt as if he were, in fact, the five feet eight inches he always told people, instead of the five feet four inches he actually was. Rubbing his hands over the soft suede, he felt like a million dollars for the first time in years. He felt so happy, he could almost forget that he was on his way to the sales meeting at Acme Insurance Company. "At least I only make appointments for the salesmen. It would be worse if I had to sell the stuff," he mumbled as he climbed aboard the number seven bus.

CHAPTER THREE

Moving more rapidly than usual, he sat on the only available seat left on the bus and lowered his head. As he opened his paper, the world spun away. He imagined himself driving the black convertible Corvette he had seen yesterday in the window of the car dealership near his office. So deep in thought, he didn't notice the tall willowy brunette that boarded the bus at the next stop, nor did he offer her his seat—at least not until he felt the high spike of her heel land squarely on his foot, her full weight bearing down on his foot. His head came up as he let out a loud yelp. "You're standing on my foot!" he squealed.

"Oh, so I am," replied the stately brunette. "You should be," she said as her penetrating black eyes met his.

Jerry squirmed trying to dislodge his foot. "I got on the bus first," he stated. He lowered his eyes, trying to ignore the stares from the rest of the passengers, but it was no use. He stood and slowly rolled up his paper, picked up his overcoat and moved out into the aisle. The brunette looked at him slyly and took his seat without even a thank you.

Jerry had the personality of a snail, except in his mind. In his mind, he was a debonair and dashing man about town, mysterious, and handsome. He didn't let reality enter into his world unless he had no other option.

Of course, at work he had to keep focused. Ever since the new manager had started, it seemed there was never time for reading the paper, long coffee breaks, or anything else. Only the phones, the everlasting phones, the nonstop dialing and pitching to uninterested prospects. What a drag life had gotten to be. He stared out the window as the bus stopped and started, picking up and letting off passengers.

Now his days were spent at "the boiler room," where he was required to make a regular number of dials per hour and set pre-figured numbers of appointments for the salespeople. He received a salary and a small commission, but the pressure was high and the management became more unsympathetic each day. Now, thoughts of getting another job and making a new life for himself crossed his mind daily. Sometimes he even looked through the help-wanted section of the paper, but he had drifted so long he couldn't seem to stop drifting. Evenings were spent in front of the television with a TV dinner and a bottle of beer for his fair. His friends had become the characters he watched on TV. He often found himself yelling at them.

He stepped off the bus and turned into the park. "Traffic was light today, so I should have a few minutes to walk in the park before work," he murmured to himself. He had taken to talking out of the side of his mouth years ago. It made him feel less conspicuous about talking to himself. He thought no one would notice it then. He didn't feel the need to rush yet, though he knew he soon would. All too soon he would begin to worry about being late for work. Willard, his boss, didn't approve of anyone being late, and he couldn't afford to draw attention to himself, especially since he hadn't made his quota for the week, and it was already Friday.

Pulling himself up to his full height, coat slung James Bond fashion over his shoulder, Jerry sauntered down the path into the park. A small breeze picked up. For a moment, the sun was gone. Clouds covered all but a sliver that lit up the box lying in the middle of the path. It was as if someone had only moments before laid it there. He almost missed it. His foot had actually hit it, making him glance down automatically.

CHAPTER FOUR

A plain brown wooden box about six inches square. It looked terribly old—as in antique, not old as in shabby. He started to pass by, but something about the box made him take a second look. Odd—the box seemed to have a glow about it. Funny, the glow seemed to seep through the pores of the wood. How curious. Jerry glanced around, forgot the time, what day it was, even where he was for a moment as he stared at the box.

There was no one around, at least none he could see or hear, and he stooped and gathered the box up into his hands to take a better look. It obviously was hollow. It was much too light to be solid, but it didn't seem to have a top, bottom, or sides to it. "How would one open it?" Jerry thought as he stared, noticing for the first time that the glow of the box had gotten brighter. "I can't even see any joints or seams in it," he mumbled to himself as he turned the box in his hands studying it. The longer he held it, the brighter it glowed, or at least the more he noticed the glow. If he set it down, the box actually appeared to quiver, almost as if it were alive.

Reluctantly, he started to put it back down on the path where he found it, knowing he was already late for work, but somehow the box called him. He couldn't leave it alone. The shining light seemed to come in waves, reaching toward him as he started along the path. Long tendrils of light stretched out to him and drew him back. He stood still, looking down at the box. Plain, brown, wooden, and very, very old, it lay there on the path silently reaching out to him with a warm, loving glow. Hell! He bent down, picked it up, and turned for home.

Time stood still, or it moved at a rate he didn't understand. Out of the corner of his eyes he could see people passing him, all going someplace. No one appeared to notice him, but that wasn't a surprise to him—they usually didn't. What surprised him most was that he could only see other people out of the corner of his eyes if he tried to look full on. It seemed he was in a vacuum. Alone in the park, it was now dark, except for a street light off in the distance.

His new overcoat lay on the ground unnoticed as he moved toward the streetlight. He wanted to study the box closer. Surprisingly, the glow didn't diminish the closer he got to the light. If anything, it appeared a little brighter.

There was something almost alive about the box, or was it the warm glow that made it seem alive. He didn't know. He only knew he had to take it home for further study.

The fact that he must have missed not only the sales meeting, but his entire day was immaterial. All that mattered was the box. Cradling the shining box in his hands as if he held something exceedingly rare and precious, he retraced his steps and ran to catch the bus with the box wrapped in his newspaper tucked under his arm.

He would avoid the lobby; fear gripped his heart at the thought of someone taking this magical box. "It's mine," Jerry murmured as he climbed the six floors to his flat, double locked his door and pulled the blinds. No one was going to see the box. He thought about calling work and telling them he had gotten sick, but it didn't seem necessary any longer. If he got fired, so what? He had the box. Its mystery was all that mattered, and he had to solve it. First, he had to find out what made it glow and how to open it.

CHAPTER FIVE

When Jerry was a little boy a friend of his had a small box from China, which didn't appear to have any opening either, but on closer inspection one did find the seam after all. Perhaps this was similar to that one. He set it on the kitchen table and examined it from all sides. Nothing. Rummaging through his desk drawer he found the magnifying glass and went back into the kitchen to try again. Nothing. There was no seam, no joining of the wood in any place that he could see on even the closest inspection. The box seemed to have been made from a single block of wood, carefully carved without even one seam or joint. Impossible! How could this be? The only thing he noticed was the glow was getting stronger. Now he started to worry. What made the glow? Could the box contain some sort of radioactive material? On the face of it, this didn't seem likely. "Don't they always put radioactive material in lead containers?"

he muttered to himself. "Wouldn't it burn through the wood? What caused the glow?"

"For Christ's sake!" he squeaked. It was only an empty box. Nothing to get worked up over, not worth the time he was spending on it.

With that thought, the glow seemed to diminish ever so slightly, and his heart sank. Why should it matter? It was only a plain old wooden box. Even as his mind formed the thought, he knew it wasn't so. There was something inside that box—or someone.

"Someone! Good Lord!" he shouted. "I'm really losing it now." Placing the box back down on his kitchen table he went to the refrigerator, pulled out a beer and sat down in front of the box to think.

"Maybe it actually is radioactive, but even if it's dangerous, I have to open it. Somehow, someway, it has to open, even if I need to break it open," Jerry muttered as he pulled a hammer out of the junk drawer and struck a heavy blow to the box. Nothing! He grabbed a screwdriver and tried pounding that into the wood with the hammer, but again nothing happened. No matter how hard he pounded the wood stood firm. Repeated blows had nicked and scarred the old metal kitchen table but made absolutely no impression on the box. None whatsoever!

The box stood unblemished. It withstood every onslaught. Nothing he did affected it, except to make the shimmering glow grow ever so slightly brighter. Jerry started to get scared. Obviously, something extremely unusual was going on here. No matter how improbable it was, the only answer he could come up with was that the box was hollowed out from the inside. Now that was impossible, but it seemed to be the truth.

If it were hollowed out from the inside, who—or what—did the hollowing? Was the hollower still inside? Was that why the light seemed to be stronger? Was the hollower still busy hollowing? What would a hollower look like if that was what was in the box?

CHAPTER SIX

He held the box up to his ear and gently shook it. Nothing. No rattle, no roll, no weight displacement. Indeed, the only noticeable effect was a nearly imperceptible flicker in the light—and flicker it did. Or did it? Was it only his imagination? Quickly, he set the box down and went to the fridge for another beer. He felt the need to have something a bit stronger than beer, but beer would have to do. Truth be known, he couldn't afford to keep anything stronger in his apartment, his wallet didn't allow it.

Chugging the second beer down, he dropped back down in his chair and gazed steadily at the box. The box glowed back at him softly in an almost comradely way. "Lord, I have been alone too long," he said to himself. "There must be a logical explanation, Jerry. Get a grip on yourself man!" he told himself.

Abruptly, he set the box back down on the table, walked back to the fridge thinking, "A ham sandwich and another bottle of beer might help me get this damn thing out of my mind." After making the sandwich, he took it and another beer, deliberately walked out of the kitchen, sat down in his large recliner, and turned on the radio. As the music filled the room, fingers of light crept around the corner and into the living room. Not actually fingers—there was no discernable outline—only the warm, pulsating glow which seemed to reach into the very marrow of his bones and draw him toward the source.

He left his sandwich and beer untouched and slowly walked back into the kitchen. The box glowed warmly at him.

"God! It's alive, and it wants me!" As though in a trance he pulled up a chair and sat down beside the table, staring into the radiance which now poured from the interior of the box.

"Who are you, and what are you?" he whispered, but the only answer he received was an increase in the intensity of the light.

Was it his imagination, or was the light getting brighter? Were the sides of the box getting thinner? Was the hollowing out still going on? Would they hollow right through the box?

Gradually, the sounds of the city outside faded away. He got up once to turn off the lights and once he heard the telephone ringing as though from a great distance. The music from the radio turned to static. However, by then he had lost all awareness of himself and the world outside. Day and night ceased to exist. No sense of hunger or thirst, weariness, or time permeated his being. All that mattered was the box and the increasing brilliance of the light. His smile grew larger until it covered his face ear to ear, and he sat there mesmerized watching the glow of the box.

When no one from work could reach him and the days went by, someone finally called the police. The officers who arrived on the scene refused to reenter the room after their first inspection, stating it felt as if something lived in that room. In the air clung a lingering smell of something sweet and wild.

The coroner's report simply stated, "Body weight, ninety-one pounds. Both eyes gone, sockets appear to have been utterly seared. Third degree burns covering his fingers and hands. The skin on his face tightly pulled back, almost as if his skin was made of plastic, and a wide, toothy smile covered his face."

There was no stench from the body, no smell of burnt flesh, and no apparent cause of the burns.

In the dust of the table, it appeared he had used his skeletal, burnt hands to trace the words.

"I love…"

www.ingramcontent.com/pod-product-compliance
Lightning Source LLC
Chambersburg PA
CBHW072233190626
46809CB00017B/1902

* 9 7 8 1 9 3 9 4 8 4 4 6 8 *